James G. Holmes

Memorials to the Memory of Mrs. Mary Amarinthia Snowden

Offered by societies, associations and Confederate camps

James G. Holmes

Memorials to the Memory of Mrs. Mary Amarinthia Snowden
Offered by societies, associations and Confederate camps

ISBN/EAN: 9783337257163

Printed in Europe, USA, Canada, Australia, Japan

Cover: Foto ©Raphael Reischuk / pixelio.de

More available books at **www.hansebooks.com**

Memorials.

To the Memory of

Mrs. Mary Amarinthia Snowden

OFFERED BY SOCIETIES, ASSOCIATIONS AND
CONFEDERATE CAMPS.

PUBLISHED BY THE

Ladies Memorial Association

Of Charleston, S. C.

A TRIBUTE TO ITS FOUNDER, AND UP TO THE TIME OF HER
DEATH ITS ONLY PRESIDENT.
A TESTIMONIAL OF LOVE AND ESTEEM OF THE MEMBERS,
TO ONE

" *Whose worth the span of rolling centuries preserves in
memory undecaying.*"

EDITED BY

JAMES G. HOLMES.

CHARLESTON, S. C.
WALKER, EVANS & COGSWELL CO., PRINTERS,
3 and 5 Broad and 117 East Bay Sts.
1898.

DEDICATED TO THE MEMORY OF

Mrs. Mary Amarinthia Snowden,

AND

Mrs. Isabell S. Snowden,

SISTERS IN THE FLESH, AND TRUE SISTERS IN

FAITH AND GOOD WORKS,

BY THE EDITOR.

MARY AMARINTHIA SNOWDEN.

She was not servant profitless; her name

"Glows on the roll which duty keeps for fame—
That golden roll with iron pen engraved,
Dipped in the heart-blood of the noble dead,
Weighed well with truthful balance, scrutinized
By eyes that love no guile and grovel not."

"The roll which duty keeps for fame" is enriched and
ennobled by the name of Mary Amarinthia Snowden. Her
co-workers of the Ladies Memorial Association, of Charleston,
have deemed it fitting that they should do their part to pre-
serve at least the words of "well done, thou good and faithful
servant," that have been put into print and published after
her death. In this spirit, and that Mrs. Snowden's beauti-
fully unselfish life, of constant endeavor for suffering
humanity, should serve as a guiding star to others, they
resolved at their annual meeting June 6th, 1898, "That the
Ladies Memorial Association, collect and publish in pamphlet
form, all of the eulogies and resolutions on the death of Mrs.
Mary Amarinthia Snowden, by which the many different
Associations, Societies and Veteran Camps have testified
through the newspapers, their tributes of love and admiration
for her noble life work."

"Also resolved, That Col. James G. Holmes be requested
to take charge of and arrange all of the matter for publica-
tion."

Deeply sensible of the honor done him, by the last clause
of the resolution, the editor of this pamphlet undertakes the
"labor of love," as one who for many years served with and
under the gifted woman, the record of whose life's work is
sought to be herein perpetuated. He brings to the task his

best efforts, and his loving, grateful appreciation of her
character and good works, such as only a Confederate Veteran can.

MARY AMARINTHIA SNOWDEN.

"Death of a truly good and great Daughter of South Carolina."

Thus The News and Courier announced the sad fact and
among the funeral notices of February 24th, 1898, we read:

"Died at her home in this city, on the afternoon of February
23d, 1898, Mary Amarinthia Snowden, widow of Wm.
Snowden, M. D."

Invitations were also published by the Ladies Memorial
Association to attend the funeral of their late President,
and also by Camp Sumter, No. 250, U. C. V. The following sketch appeared in The News and Courier at the same
time:

There is a beatitude of the faithful dead, uttered from the
Heaven to which they have passed, as truly as there is a
beatitude of the saintly living, spoken upon that earth through
which they strive. If the Son of God utters His blessing
upon the one from the Holy Mount, the Spirit of God pro-
claims the blessedness of the other from the very skies where
it is made real. He says of them: "They rest from their
labors, and their works do follow them."

And this is the beautiful and impressive epitaph which has
written itself in every thought with the first tidings that Mrs.
Mary Amarinthia Snowden has ceased from among the living.
Rest from labor, and that labor always and ungrudgingly for
others, could not conceivably come to her but with the cessa-
tion of life itself. For many years past, infirmity of health,
advancing age and many trials conspired to make effort hard,
and the necessity of respite seemingly imperative, but the

strong spirit has overcome them all, so that up to the very last of life the great interests and tasks to which she consecrated her life received unceasing attention, supervision and unwearying effort.

It would require far more time, thought, research and a calmer spirit than can be summoned now, in the shock of this great bereavement, even to outline the wonderful and abiding things which this noble lady has accomplished for her city, her State, and the cause of the Confederacy, which she held so sacred, right and dear. It might be fitly said of her: "Do you seek her monument? Look around!" The fund which built the Calhoun Monument owes its preservation through the war to the devotion and intrepidity of Mrs. Snowden, and her equally consecrated sister, Mrs. Isabella S. Snowden. The beautiful shaft that stands to the great Senator on Marion Square is almost, if not quite, equally a monument to these heroic and self-sacrificing sisters. The lot in Magnolia Cemetery, where sleep a thousand Confederate soldiers, was secured largely through their efforts, and the head stones at each soldier's grave. The Confederate dead brought thither from Gettysburg would still be sleeping there but for Mrs. Snowden's unresting, unceasing and patriotic piety. The Ladies Memorial Association, which decorates the graves yearly, was largely founded by her.

So many and great have been the works wrought by this single life, consecrated to usefulness, that each seems greatest until another is contemplated. But the "Home for Mothers, Widows and Daughters of Confederate Soldiers," is the achievement which cost most supreme exertion and has exerted the widest influence. It has existed and flourished for thirty years, and has supported and educated more than a thousand young Confederate orphans. The first institution of the kind in the South, it bids fair to outlive all others. It is fixed upon a sound financial basis, and is seated in public confidence and regard.

That the place of Mrs. Snowden can be filled in the enterprises of benevolence which she started and carried forward no one dares to hope. Yet she laid down her work in them at a time when, if ever, they could promise perpetuity and prosperity. Calmly contemplating and fully providing for "the last of earth," she fell asleep yesterday and passed to where her "works will follow her."

Mary Amarinthia Snowden (nee Yates) was born at Charleston, S. C., September 10th, 1819. Her parents were of English and German extraction, and had settled in South Carolina before the Revolution of 1776. Her father died when she was 18 months old, and her bringing up devolved upon the mother, from whom she inherited that stern inflexibility of purpose, common sense and public spirit which has enabled her to inaugurate and carry on successfully so many good works in her native State.

At that time the schools of Charleston for female education were not of the best, and her mother, being in affluent circumstances, moved with the family to Philadelphia, Pa., for the education of the children. There they remained five years, when they returned to South Carolina. Two of her brothers were sent to Scotland to complete their education, and she went to the Seminary of Dr. Elias Marks, at Barhamville, near Columbia, S. C., a school of high grade, which, for sixty years, threw open its doors to the daughters of the best families of the State. At school, although not the first in her class, she conducted herself creditably, and was beloved alike by teachers and scholars for her keen intelligence, perfect sincerity, playful wit and charming esprit, characteristics which did not fade, but merely mellowed by age and adversity. She made friends from all parts of the State, not the evanescent friendships which generally mark school girl life, but those cemented by time, mutual hopes, fears and sufferings. Her maidenhood was spent most enjoyably; now at the balls and festivities of winter life in the city, and then on some old plantation among those planters who, in lettered ease, passed their days and years, and furnished a noble type of American manhood which has perished with its corner stone, slavery. At Columbia she met the leaders of public opinion, men who eventually dared all, and lost all, save honor, for conscience sake. Among her most intimate acquaintances were Senators Calhoun and Elmore, Governor David Johnson, Judges Earle and Aldrich, and the Hon. W. L. Yancey, the prime mover of secession. Perhaps the first institution with which she was connected was the "School Ship Lodebar," of Charleston, which owed its origin to the exertions of her brother, the Rev. Wm. B. Yates. It is believed to have been the first of its kind in the world. Here the homeless vagabonds, which are to be found in every city, were trained in all the duties of the sailor's life, and at the same time received a good English education on board ship.

"The good men do" is accretive; encouraged by the success attained by the Charleston school ship, such institutions have sprung up in nearly every large port in the United States and Great Britain. In 1857 Miss Yates was married to William Snowden, M. D., of a highly respectable family of South Carolina planters. Of this union there have been two children.

Soon after the death of Mr. Calhoun, the great statesman of the South, and the especial pride of South Carolina, an association was organized for the purpose of erecting a suitable monument to his memory, "tanto nomini nullum par elogium," but this monument is intended to inform posterity of the love and admiration his people bore him. His works, those "sacred oracles of political wisdom," constitute his most enduring monument. In this work Mrs. Snowden took a prominent part; during the night of the burning of Columbia the assets of the Association were worn on the persons of Mrs. Snowden and an equally devoted sister. Governor Porter and Col. Gaillard declared in the public prints that through the efforts of Mrs. Snowden the Calhoun Monument Association had proportionately preserved more of its funds during that devastating war than any corporation of the South.

In 1861 there came the War of Secession, and here Mrs. Snowden's character shines in its brightest light. Numerous hospitals along its beleaguered coast owed their existence to her endeavors; provisions and clothing were sent weekly to the armies of Virginia and the West; she undertook an expedition to Warrenton, Va., ten miles from the battlefield of Manassas, at the time of the second battle, over frightful roads (the railways being destroyed by the enemy) and almost impassable rivers; though advised of the danger, carrying with her clothing and comforts for the wounded, and personally attending the dying in the hospitals, at private houses, and on an open field on Academy Hill. Among these last were one hundred and eighty South Carolinians.

Under her supervision, and with the aid of other patriotic ladies, a bazaar was opened in Columbia, S. C., which contributed $350,000 to the Confederacy. Special recognition of her services was made by the Congress of the Confederate States by allowing her to import, as best she could, through the blockade, wines and liquors of all sorts for the Southern hospitals. She was present, with her family, in Columbia, S. C., during the sack and burning of that city by the army of General Sherman. Many hundred Confederate prisoners, without means, and generally too weak for transportation, were under her care for some months. With the contributions of the citizens, and what she could extort from the Federal forces, these men were clothed and fed until they could return to their homes. The halls of the University of the State were put at her disposal, and here, with a few friends and her former slaves (the majority of whom had refused to follow in the wake of the victorious army), did she exhibit that executive ability and faculty for organization which gave her rank among the first women of the State.

With shattered hopes (for what Southener ever doubted ultimate success? so firmly were they convinced of the justice of their cause), the loss of a noble and devoted husband, property depreciated to one-tenth its real value, and a family dependent on her for support, did she return to Charleston, in 1865.

But "the cause," though lost, was none the less dear. At Magnolia, the City of the Dead, lie the remains of over eight hundred volunteers who had fallen in defence of the city. With several friends, she, in 1866, formed a Memorial Association; from the funds raised by this body have been erected eight hundred marble head stones, with their name, rank and State engraved thereon, and a statue in bronze of a Confederate soldier surmounts the granite column which stands in the centre of the enclosure.

But in honoring the dead, the living were not to be forgotten; and in 1867 she bent her energies towards preparing a Home for the Mothers, Widows and Daughters of Confederate soldiers. This Institution, the only one of its kind in the Southern States, was founded in 1867. One dollar from a widow in Baltimore was the first donation. Widows and mothers of Confederate soldiers are here allowed a home, and daughters are educated for a merely nominal sum, or as their means allow. Hundreds of the impoverished daughters of South Carolina have been educated at this Institution, and many a widow and mother has found there a "home and a resting place." Seventy thousand dollars have been raised for its support since its inception. When the design was barely digested, and its novelty had made the public doubtful of its ultimate success, Mrs. Snowden never hesitated a moment; but, with her sister, mortgaged their own residence for payment of the first year's rent on the building. But friends came forward, subscriptions to the good work increased, and the rent was paid. The building is now owned by the Association, and the nucleus of a handsome endowment fund is in the banks.

Not only did Mrs. Snowden interest herself in most schemes for the public good, but she was highly honored at home for those little unnumbered acts of kindness which make life worth living to the thoughtful. That she had not the reputation of a Florence Nightingale, or Burdett Coutts, is granted. There are claimed for her none of those great acts of Christian philanthropy which only riches make possible, but in her native State she was known far and wide as one who had worked since her youth for the benefit of others, with no reward save the consciousness of duty well performed, and what Milton calls "the dear affection of the public good."

Editorially The News and Courier wrote :

"I cannot forbear to allude to the venerable and beloved Carolina matron, who, amid all the perils of war and the storms of battle, carried, concealed on her person, the sacred fund which was dedicated to the erection of this monument."

In concluding his masterly address at the dedication of the Calhoun Monument, in this city, in April, 1887, the Hon. L. Q. C. Lamar paid this high tribute to the splendid woman who passed away yesterday to her everlasting reward. The monument on Marion Square is a monument not only to the great statesman, whose memory it perpetuates, but it is a monument as well to the builders, and to none more surely and truly than Mrs. M. A. Snowden, who now rests from her labors.

We shall never see her like again. Her life was spent in the service of others. There was not a day which did not record some kindly act, some blessed counsel, some generous deed, some inspiring sentiment. Whether ministering in the wayside hospital, during the war, or caring for the children of the Southern soldiers, or striving to perpetuate the memories of the glorious past, or laying fresh flowers on the graves of the deathless dead, her life was a blessing, her example an inspiration.

The city where she had always lived, the State which she loved with unspeakable devotion, and the people whom she served to almost the last moment of her earthly existence, may well mourn her loss. She will not return, nor would we call her back from the peaceful sleep which the Almighty gives to His beloved. Words are weak, and grief is unavailing, and tears are idle—only the eye of faith and love can appreciate the height and depth, the glory unapproachable and everlasting of the larger life upon which the departed has entered.

Editorial notices also appeared in The Greenville News, The Hampton County Guardian, and other papers of the State, all couched in the spirit of admiration for her proven worth.

The News and Courier of February 25th contained this account of the funeral :

The funeral services over the remains of the late Mrs. M. A. Snowden were conducted at the French Huguenot Church yesterday afternoon, at 4.30 o'clock. The seating capacity of the church was totally inadequate to accommodate the throng of people who gathered to pay the last token of respect to the memory of a woman who was known throughout the city for her good deeds. Many persons were forced to stand in the aisles throughout the services, and there were still others who remained outside of the church.

The coffin was borne into the church and subsequently to the grave by the following pallbearers : Daniel Ravenel, A. L. Yates, St. Julien Yates, Julius DuBose, James G. Snowden, Dr. W. P. Porcher, H. P. Blackman, W. H. Porter and Minott Gaillard.

The honorary pallbearers were: Judge W. H. Brawley, Dr. R. L. Brodie, Dr. F. L. Parker, Mr. Charles Snowden, Col. James G. Holmes, Mr. A. Markley Lee, Mr. Clarence Cunningham, Mr. W. H. Porter, and Mr. S. G. Pinckney. The honorary pallbearers preceded the casket into the church, and following it were a number of the United Confederate Veterans, led by General C. I. Walker. The casket was covered with handsome floral tributes. As the procession advanced up the aisle the services for the dead in the Huguenot Church were opened with the chanting of Psalms. The services were conducted by Dr. Brackett, of the Second Presbyterian Church; Dr. Vedder, of the Huguenot Church; and Dr. Cuthbert, of the First Baptist Church, in a most impressive manner. The hymns sung were: "Art Thou Weary; Art Thou Languid," and "Jesus, Lover of My Soul." In the former the congregation joined, while the latter was rendered as a recessional.

Before reading that part of the service assigned to him, Dr. Vedder said that it was not the custom of the church to speak of its dead until the Sunday following a funeral, but he felt sure that in that instance he was authorized in violating the rule. Continuing, he said:

In the last discourse preached from this pulpit a contrast was drawn between the manner in which some different persons meet the last enemy. Some claim, in the language of the prophet, to have made a covenant with death, and to be at agreement with all that shall follow it; the covenant with death as to what they shall think of it, usually determining not to think of it at all, or if compelled to do so, not to fear it.

But is fearlessness a pillar upon which they can rest their hopes ? Is indifference or defiance a right greeting for this universal visitant ?

Shall a man pass his life here hardly and laboriously, and have nothing to show for it in the end but this ? Shall a man have every element and condition of happiness here, and no surety of happiness hereafter ? But even in any close of life there must be something of introspection. Some inventory of that business of life now about to be closed up forever; some search into the storehouse of memories which wait to be ministries of regret or remorse. Some couches there are where the reaper comes to a smiling harvest, where the wing of the death angel fans a placid brow, and its hand touches a tranquil pulse; when death's summons is the welcome enfranchisement of a fettered spirit; some there have been who fully weighed all the felicities of life, or its purposes broken off, and yet have said with the dying Senator in the Senate House: "This is the last of earth; I am content."

The pastor did not anticipate that such a close of life would be practically exemplified in his own communion before another Sabbath dawned; yet thus it has been. The life which has now and here reached its bound had long foreseen and provided for this hour. In every detail the scene of which we now make part had passed before its vision. The frail house of life which the Great Builder has now taken down was set fully in order. Calmly, peacefully, trustfully, it was exchanged for the house not made with hands, eternal in the heavens.

It was a beautiful parable of old which represented man as possessed of three friends:one was greatly prized; the second tenderly loved; and the third more lightly esteemed. But when man's last hour had come, the first friend, who had been held so highly, forsook him with his last breath; the second friend, so dearly loved, accompanied him to the portals of the tomb, but could go no further; but the third friend was with him as the support of his last hours, went with him into the tomb, and into all the life beyond to make it glad. It need hardly be said that the first friend was wealth, which a man must leave behind; the second friend, family, which can only go with him to the tomb; and the third friend is faith, with its motive of love to God, and ministry of love to man. He, in whom this faith is the inspiration and energy of life, can say:

For this poor form,
Which vests me in, I give it to destruction
As gladly as the storm-beat traveller
Who, having reached his destined place of shelter,
Drops at the door his mantle's cumbrous weight.

Just prior to the opening of the services, the Rev. Dr. A. Toomer Porter, of the Church of the Holy Communion, passed up the aisle and laid a beautiful bunch of carnations upon the casket. The church was so much crowded that Dr. Vedder invited Dr. Porter within the railing about the pulpit. At the conclusion of the services the Benediction was pronounced by Dr. Porter, most impressively.

The interment was made in the family lot in Magnolia Cemetery. While the grave was being filled in the young ladies of the Confederate Home School, who had attended the services at the church in a body, sang several hymns, among them being "Just As I Am," "Safe in the Arms of Jesus," and "Asleep in Jesus, Blessed Sleep."

March the 1st, the Ladies' Memorial Association of Charleston, S. C , whose founder, and at the time of her death, only President, Mrs. Snowden had been, passed the following resolutions:

Whereas, it is a very sad duty which now calls us together, for with tender and reverent hands we would lay a chaplet of loving thoughts and memories upon the grave of our late President, Mrs. Mary Amarinthia Snowden, a noble Christian woman, whose life was dedicated to kind deeds and grand enterprises for the benefit of friends, city, Confederates, living and dead, without one thought of herself. From mountains to seaboard her loss has caused deep sorrow; long will her memory be revered and cherished. This Memorial Association, the first 'one organized in the South, owes much of its founding and prosperity to her untiring efforts, large sympathies and wise management, which we, her associates, have ever keenly appreciated. Therefore, be it

Resolved, That this Memorial Association has met with an irreparable loss in the death of Mrs. M. Amarinthia Snowden, for long years its President, faithful officer, and the Board of Directors an earnest, sincere friend.

2. That we continue as a sacred trust the work she loved so well, in caring for the graves of our Confederate dead, and raising monuments to their memories.

3. That on Memorial Day we will all wear, with our badges, a black ribbon, in token of respect for her memory

4. That we offer our sincere sympathy to the family of our late President, Mrs. M. A. Snowden, in their deep affliction, mourning with them for her who has received her reward: "Well done, good and faithful servant, enter thou into the joy of thy Lord." Also that a copy of these resolutions be sent to the family, and published in The News and Courier.

The following was then offered and adopted:

Resolved, That in token of our regret for the loss of our beloved President, Mrs. Mary Amarinthia Snowden, this Association proceed immediately to take action for the erection of a permanent memorial to her character and work.

Resolved, That a committee of three be appointed to suggest and report to this Association the form and place for this memorial, and the method by which the means for it may be best secured.

Resolved, That the collection taken up on next Memorial Day be exclusively devoted to this purpose.

On the same day the "Board of Control" of the "Home for Mothers, Widows and Daughters of Confederate Soldiers and Sailors" passed these resolutions:

Whereas, It has pleased God to remove from the scene of her earthly service our beloved President, to whom, under His providence, the Confederate Home of Charleston owes its origin, continuance, usefulness and prosperity; and

Whereas, This bereavement, so often feared, comes at last so suddenly as to forbid calm thought and speech; and

Whereas, This first meeting of the Board of Control after her departure may not pass without some expression of our grief, however broken and feeble. Therefore, be it

Resolved, That the demise of Mrs. Mary Amarinthia Snowden, over which the city and State, which she so devotedly loved, mourn as a public loss, comes to us, her associates, with the overwhelming force of a personal and irreparable calamity.

Resolved, That we bow submissively to the Divine hand from which this dispensation comes, acknowledging the mercy of the same gracious Hand in giving us so long the consecrated life of our sister, and the inspiration of her zeal, energy and tirelessness in all good works.

Resolved, That we accept as a sacred trust the work in which she was so long our leader, and which she has left to us in a state of such efficiency and stability that any success which shall attend our administration of its affairs will only be a tribute to her wisdom, ardor and efficiency.

Resolved, That we will treasure her memory with the tenderest devotion as one whom it was a privilege to know, and with whom it will always be our pride and honor to have been associated in the service of Confederate sympathy and helpfulness.

Resolved, That our dearest and truest sympathies be extended to the children of our President, who only echo the voice of a community and Commonwealth when they "rise up and call their mother blessed."

J. A. ADGER, Chairman.
A. SIMPSON.
MRS. C. S. VEDDER.

Editorially The Southern Christian Advocate, March 3rd, 1898, wrote:

*   *   *   *   *   *   *

"Mrs. Snowden was a remarkable woman, and she rendered very great service. A Southerner of Southerners, a Confederate of Confederates, she devoted her life to distinctively Southern and Confederate ideas. The monument to Calhoun, the Ladies' Memorial Association, the Confederate section in Magnolia Cemetery, with its hero-dead, the Confederate Home and School, all speak eloquently of the thoughts that ruled a brave, loving and unchangeable heart. This consecration of

purpose made possible the large results of her endeavor.
Such character and life as Mrs. Snowden's should be held
before the generations as an inspiration and an example.
* * * * * Mrs Snowden was the incarnation of
Southern womanhood in the war between the States and after."

The most important and impressive services in memory of
the honored and lamented dead were the Memorial Services
held at the Huguenot Church, the church of her tenderest
love and devotion, Sunday, March 6th, 1898. The News
and Courier of the next day contains this account of the
solemn and heartfelt services:

The Rev. Charles S. Vedder, D. D., pastor of the Huguenot Church, preached a memorial discourse at the morning
service, on the life and work of the late Mrs. M. A. Snowden. Dr. Vedder was associated with much of Mrs. Snowden's work for more than thirty years, and was her pastor
during all that time. He was acquainted, therefore, with
her work, and he spoke feelingly of her character and her
career.

Dr. Vedder's text was from John 11, 3:

"Then took Mary a pound of ointment, of spikenard, very
precious, and anointed the feet of Jesus, and wiped His feet
with her hair, and the house was filled with the odor of the
ointment."

These words, said the minister, call us to look upon a scene
ineffably pathetic and memorable—a scene the circumstances
of which are so true to nature that they could not have been
invented; a scene in which gratitude manifests itself in abso-
lute consonance with the differences of human temperament
and estimate. The place is Bethany, and the home of Simon,
the leper. Seated at his hospitable board, a guest only less
welcome than the Lord Jesus Himself, is Lazarus, whom He
had raised from the dead. Thought is left to conceive, for

2

words cannot portray, the emotion which thrills his heart as he looks upon his Deliverer, and hears again the voice which woke him from the sleep of the tomb. Simon, recalled from the desert places to which he had been banished as a leper, and restored to home and family, gave natural token of his gratitude by welcoming his Healer to a feast in that home and with that family. But still another was present, and her grateful love found far other expression. With ointment of spikenard, very precious, she anointed the feet of Jesus, and wiped His feet with the hair of her head.

Two of these forms of gratitude passed without cavil. That the restored, the resurrected brother, should look upon his Lord with a depth of feeling that forbade utterance, that Simon should signalize his ransom from worse than death by honor shown to his Deliverer; these things could be understood and approved. But that the gentle sister should bring an offering seemingly far, far beyond her means, or which implied a lavish self-denial and sacrifice, was held to be by some of the disciples a needless and unjustifiable waste.

Their censure received instant and earnest reproof...That this reproof may come echoing down through the ages the beautiful incident of which it forms part —not otherwise specially significant—is embalmed in our Gospels. With that care which our Scripture has to make duties and privileges about which debate may circle, so certain by illustration that all intelligent debate may be silenced, the offering of Mary has emphatic approval—its human criticism is of record, in order to be condemned.

Men have been, and some men are now, ready to sit in judgment upon all those forms of service to Christ which express themselves in what are called extremes. If this judgment be warranted, then the martyrdom of Stephen, of the early apostles and disciples; of all the victims of heathen persecution; of the scaffolds and stake welcomed to maintain Christ's crown and covenant;. the persecution unto death or banishment of those whom this Church commemorates; the glad immolation of missionaries upon the altar of fatal climates to preach Jesus! all these things and things like them are a needless, suicidal waste. And because even such a judgment is possible, and that from some of His own disciples, our Lord has set the seal of His own encomium upon the offering of Mary of Bethany What He said of it we learn more fully from the Gospels, which record a like incident. Shall we recall His commendation: He said: "Why trouble ye her? She hath wrought a good work upon Me."

What was there in this act of affection and honor which entitled it to the exalted praise, uttered by Divine lips, that it was a "good work?" Does not the encomium seem disproportioned to the act? Was it more than any woman of Bethany would have gladly done to Him who was honored and beloved? The Saviour Himself answers the question.

It was a "good work" in respect to the time in which it was wrought. As if by the prophetic instinct of true devotion, or, perhaps, taught better than His disciples by the words of His own lips, many knew that the Lord was to be but a little time with them. A few days more—the coming event had cast its sombre shadow before, and in it she seemed to walk—a few days more, and she, with the other women, should stand by His cross, beholding an agony which they should be powerless to assuage. Other opportunity to honor Him might never be afforded. If, as He said, He should rise again, would the conqueror of death and the grave be the same as now, accessible, sympathetic, loving? Would He still be the friend of the lowly, sitting at meat in their homes, and identified with their sorrows?

"She has come aforehand to anoint My body for the burying," said Jesus, in commending what His disciples, or some of them, condemned. It might, perhaps, be thought that these words were prompted by profound and delicate consideration for the woman, shrinking under the harsh censures of His disciples, rather than as expressing a valid reason for the act which they sanctioned. Though this view might do no dishonor to Him who spake the words, it cannot be justified. His words more than imply that she had presentiment of the significance and timeliness of the offering she bore. The fulness of its meaning has not been explained to us, save that it was an "anointing beforehand." It was the custom of all nations to adorn the sacrifices for the altar. It was meet, then, that He who was the supreme victim of all sacrifice— the substance of all the shadows of vicarious suffering— should be anointed for His one perfect oblation. Those by whom He should be slain would crown Him with thorns, and not garlands; cover Him with reproach, not reverential glory; and it was seemly that dear and devoted hands should anticipate the beautiful offices which affection should be denied at His cross.

Our Lord, moreover, was the Priest, as well as the Propitiation, and the simple act of the woman did but symbolize that anointing of God which He had received, and by which He was solemnly set apart to offer the sacrifice of His own body for sin.

It was a "good work," in that she had done "what she could."

Being a woman, it was not permitted her to share the immediate trials and privations of her Lord. She could not be with Him always, like the twelve, showing devotion in nameless ways. The words of the Master warrant the belief that the ointment was her all. Whether she had expended all to purchase it, or whether it had been treasured as the memento of better days, we are not told. One or other of these suppositions is probably true.

Simon, the leper, might have presented the same offering, without challenging comment. Possessed of such wealth as enabled him to be hospitable, he could have given something more costly without sacrificing a single luxury or comfort. It might well have been nothing compared with what he could do. With Mary it was "what she could." Like the two mites of the widow, she sought with personal and extreme sacrifice to embalm the body so dear to her for burial. The

Saviour accepted the offering, and promised it undying remembrance.

Included in His words also is the enunciation of the principles that holy impulse buildeth better than it knows. The murmuring of the disciples at what seemed a needless waste was natural. They thought their censure charitable and humane. Judas, who seems to be foremost in complaint, uttered this thought, and the rest tacitly consented. What must have been their surprise at the rebuke? "They measured moral quality by practical utility." Jesus taught them that the true estimate of an act is the motive which prompts the spirit by which it is pervaded.

The mind is many-voiced—the heart has but a single speech. Cold reason often shuts close the door of mercy, which affectionate impulse would throw wide open. When a compassionate spirit says "give," a calculating reason hesitates, lest it should give amiss. There may be nothing blame-worthy in the delay. There is a place for carefulness in giving. That remarkable book, dating back to the second century, which was found and translated a few years ago, and aroused a world-wide interest, "The Teaching of the Twelve Apostles," has this forcible saying: "Let thine alms sweat in thine hand until thou knowest to whom thou shouldst give." Indiscriminate and promiscuous benevolence is not building well, but ill—it is rather not building at all, but breaking up the foundations of self-respect and self-support. But the lesson of our subject is that there is a time and place when and where we may not stop for hard and curious questioning to stem the tide of impulsive feeling, when it would flow forth in a flood which reason would call waste. Sensibility to others' woes has been truly called

"A sudden sense of right,
An hasty conscience, reason's blushing morn,
Instinctive kindness, ere reflections born;
Prompt sense of equity to thee belongs
The swift redress of unexamined wrongs,
Eager to serve the cause perhaps untried,
But always swift to choose the suffering side."

There are times, and our subject warns us to give them heed, when if at no time else, "reason is progressive, but instinct is complete; swift instinct leaps, slow reason feebly climbs."

You need not be told, brethren, to what end these lessons of the text have been gathered. Another Mary has passed from us, who poured the ointment of an absolutely devoted life upon her Saviour's feet—the "spikenard very precious" of an unresting ministry to others in His name, and for His sake. Public testimony of every kind has said of these now folded hands that they did "what they could." But the Church which she loved so well, and served so long, cannot let these suffice. It claims the right and exercises the privilege of laying its own tribute upon the altar of her memory. If the act of the Mary of the Scripture record was to be embalmed in everlasting remembrance, the life which has been lived among our own, and which that suggests, should not pass without grateful recognition by the generation which it served.

Turn back to that page of time which tells of our immediate history nearly a third of a century gone. Look upon that Southern land which had been a garden of beauty, laid waste by sword and fire; upon a people cultured, refined, chivalric, brave, sensitive to honor and enamored of right, crushed now in the utter disappointment of confident hopes, shorn of all civil immunities, reduced to abject poverty, and subjected to a rule ignorant, insolent, rapacious and vulgarly oppressive beyond words. See lawlessness intrenching itself in the form of law; brigandage organizing itself in the Legislature of once proud and honored commonwealths: the ermine of the judicial bench, spotless through all its history before, smirched, stained, befouled with every form of defilement. Former enmity stood aghast at the sight, and wrote its verdict of the change by calling the Palmetto the "Prostrate State." Those fearful days have now become a shuddering memory, and are only recalled that we may recall the heroic life which met them and wrung from their dread hours sublime achievements.

At the very core of the ruin of that time was the hopeless future. Mothers, widowed by the war, were often without a roof under which they could hide their tears from those who mocked them; sisters, made brotherless, and helpless, looked out upon life with unrelieved despair; daughters, tenderly reared, wrought in the fields to eke out scant subsistence for the body, whilst their minds could not dream of cultivation. The incredible prospect loomed forth of a people whose reverence for their women had passed into an axiom, and whose women had been generally worthy of their proud regard—of such a people confronting the coming years with a generation of their daughters, outside of the cities, without the simplest and most rudimentary elements of the knowledge which would give grace to their lives and fitness for its inevitable responsibilities.

It was a condition which appalled contemplation, and yet which seemed inescapable. Men struggled vainly even to conceive, much more to achieve, the means of relief. Ministers at God's altar, as they confessed openly and unashamed—for the problem appeared to defy solution—ministers of the Gospel, who sought to move first in a work which so peculiarly belonged to their office, despairingly acknowledged defeat.

And then—it is the simple truth—a gentle woman, fragile in body, but fearless in soul—wearing the weeds of her own widowhood; one who had before organized agencies of supply for the soldiers in the field, whilst the strife lasted, and ministered untiringly in the hospitals for the sick and wounded; one whose belief in the sacredness of the cause which had failed, made its loss an incurable woe—such a woman refused to be daunted by the failures and doubts and discouragements of others.

Before the thought had taken form anywhere else in the devastated land, this Mary, with her Martha—sister—save that this Martha, unlike the Martha of the Scripture record, was as eager to sit at the feet of her Master to learn, as she gladly cumbered herself with much serving for Him—conceived and carried into immediate effect the plan of a shelter for other widowed hearts.

The story is as familiar, perhaps, as household words. But can we ever weary of the recital? The present speaker was honored in being a witness and humble participant in the first steps—though only as the pastor, who was asked to be present with counsel and sympathy, and not with any hope or claim of other association with its actual work, though he has had glad share in its after operation. With one dollar, and that the gift of a widow in a distant city, to pay the rental, a spacious building was secured, at an annual cost of $1,700, and these two sisters mortgaged their own and only home to secure the rental. With undelaying promptness the place was prepared and its doors thrown open, and twenty-five claimants of Confederate sympathy were received. An organization was instantly formed, and the present Constitution, in all its essential features, was adopted. Of the thirteen ladies who formed the first Board of Control, only two now survive.

None who were present will ever forget the scene when the Home was formally inaugurated. A hush, as in the very presence of the dead, rested upon the vast assemblage which thronged the Home parlors. Ministers of many denominations—two of the most eminent of which have now passed away, the beloved Christopher Gadsden and Edwin T. Winkler—took part in the impressive service, and besought that Divine favor upon the holy enterprise which has attended it ever since.

A school was established at first, but only for the children of the inmates, and twenty-five pupils were taught by the glad and gratuitous service of young ladies of the city. Within six months the Home sheltered seventy permanent inmates, and the school had more than fifty pupils. Then thirteen young ladies were received and boarded, under the care of an experienced matron, and enabled to attend some of the best schools in the city. In the year following, the number of young ladies was increased to twenty-five, and of the inmates to one hundred and two. At the third anniversary both of these numbers had increased, and the plan was inaugurated, which has ever since been carried out—of not only furnishing a home for the pupils, but of providing the means and opportunity of education, under competent teachers, within the institution itself. From that day to this there has been an average of fifty-two pupils annually in the Home and its school—the number in one year alone reaching as high as eighty-seven. And these young ladies have borne some of the best names in Carolina's history. Not only does the Home own the building which it first rented, but has added to it as much more, and has invested scholarships in many endeared names. And it has sheltered for years very many widows and sisters of Confederate soldiers.

And it is no exaggeration to say that not a single one of these great results would have been possible or probable, but for the noble sisters, who, under God, gave not a portion, but the whole of their lives to it—one falling by the way, a sacrifice to her work, and the other but now resting from her labors. To her full surrender of time, thought and strength to its interests; to her indomitable, unslumbering purpose, zeal, patience, persistence and faith; to her example, inspiring others who have wrought with her, grandly and effectively; to her determination to do "what she could," we owe an enterprise of pious, patriotic and practical moment, whose influence eternity alone can measure.

Far, far more than once or thrice has it been said, and that not by cavillers, but even by comrades in like work, "Why was the waste of the ointment of this precious life made, which might have been sold for the price of less laborious days and service in other spheres?" But none will ask this question now. And He who knows that all this was done for Him, the impulse of an affection which took no counsel of cold reason in fearing failure; He who said: "Inasmuch as ye have done it unto the least of these, ye have done it unto Me." He will say: "She hath done what she could; she hath wrought a good work upon Me."

And she of whom this record is true, had been worthy of imperishable remembrance among her own people, even if it could never have been written. The custodian of a great treasure of securities, representing a large sum of money, she bore them safely throughout all her journeying, ministerings and ceaseless labors, through four years of war—bore them, she or her noble sister, alternately, next their person, in constant peril of robbery, and even of loss of life, and delivered them up at the end undiminished in number and value— the only wealth that fully survived the conflict—and then rested not until they had fulfilled their purpose. The beautiful shaft which stands in our city to Carolina's illustrious statesman, is no less a memorial to her whose fearless faithfulness made it possible.

Nor did her zeal alone include in its scope the widowed and orphaned survivors of the war. With kindred souls, she cared for the dust of those who had fallen in it—the calm sleepers who lie in our Magnolia, sentineled by the almost breathing statue which keeps guard over their serried ranks, had rested in unknown, unmarked, and even in distant and unregarded graves, where no tribute flowers nor loving words would keep them in remembrance, but mediately, if not immediately, for her who could not rest till their native skies bent above these dead, and loving hands could deck their tombs.

Over her sepulchre, if over any that our history has known, may be written, as a single sentence, which is a whole biography of sublime service; written as the rebuke of every fear to undertake what needs to be done because of seeming impossibility; written as the encomium of the highest life. "She hath done what she could."

March 13th, The News and Courier published some beautiful verses written by Miss E. B. Cheeseborough, who, after many years of absence, is home again; perhaps Mrs. Snowden's oldest living friend; and they appear in full in the tribute to Mrs. Snowden, delivered at the Memorial Services May 10th, at Magnolia Cemetery.

March 15th, the Gentlemen's Auxiliary Association paid their tribute to worth in these words:

Whereas, It has pleased God to take from our midst and recall to His heavenly fold the spirit of our late President, Mary Amarinthia Snowden; be it

Resolved, That we, the Gentlemen's Auxiliary Association to the Board of Control of the Home for the Mothers, Widows and Daughters of Confederate Soldiers, humbly bow to the will of the Almighty, and that in her demise we recognize our loss of a living example in and perpetual inspiration to that actual self abnegation which calls to earth and gives practical action to the holy three, Hope, Faith and Charity; that in her demise we have lost an ardent, untiring, unflinching leader in that work which brings in all of its tangibility relief to those in want, alleviation to the suffering, comfort to those in sorrow, a renewal of hope to the dejected, and upon which God has set His seal of approval; and that while we will ever strive to imitate her lofty character, we yet feel our inability to realize in its fulness her high, pure and unselfish nature.

Resolved, That we offer our deepest sympathy to the Board of Control of the Home for the Mothers, Widows and Daughters of Confederate Soldiers, who in her demise have lost a leader and co-worker of the highest intellectual and executive ability, of the most sagacious judgment, of the wisest counsel, and of a most encouraging and inspiring temperament; one ever ready by self-denial, personal courage, and willing responsibility to give that moral support so necessary in life's battle for the achievement of good works.

Resolved, That we offer our deepest sympathy to the mothers, widows and daughters of Confederate soldiers, who in her demise have lost one nearer to them than a patroness, a mother who dedicated the noblest impulses of her heart, the strongest and most absorbing reflections of her mind, the greatest energies of her physical being, and the most valuable moments of her time to their bodily comfort as well as their mental and spiritual development and welfare, that by their more elevated lives they could better illustrate and reflect the image of their Maker and the most glorious work of God.

Resolved, That we offer our deepest sympathy to her bereaved children, who in her demise have lost the ever present companionship of that tenderest love, most responsive sympathy, deepest interest, and most subtle appreciation, which is to be found only in a mother's heart.

Resolved, That a page of our Minute Book be dedicated to her memory.

Resolved, That we erect in a suitable place in the Confederate Home building a marble mural tablet, not only as a mark of our deepest respect, reverence and gratitude for the great work the Confederate Home commemorates, but as a memorial to one who, in consecrating the measure of her days to the actual application of God's command to feed, clothe and shelter the needy, and by mental and moral training, to enlighten, expand and exalt the soul, has proved herself to be the highest type of woman and a friend to all mankind.

> CLARENCE CUNNINGHAM.
> ZIMMERMAN DAVIS.
> S. G. STONEY.

The next in order of resolutions in honor of the late Mrs. Snowden, are those, of peculiar beauty, passed by the Charleston Chapter, United Daughters of the Confederacy, March 19th, 1898 :

The members of Charleston Chapter, Daughters of the Confederacy, are called upon to place on record their sense of the loss they sustained in the death, on the 23d of February last, of Mrs. Mary Amarinthia Snowden, in the 79th year of her age.

Most of the members of this Chapter derive their claims to membership from the reflected deeds of others, but our departed friend needed no record of distinguished service of father, husband or brother to entitle her name to be written high up on our roll. During the struggle for the establishment of our loved Southern Confederacy she devoted herself to deeds of tender help and sympathy to our sick and wounded soldiers, nursing them in her own home, sharing with them every comfort which she herself enjoyed, or visiting them with daily ministrations of food and delicacies in the crowded hospitals, carrying to them also words of cheer and hope, and helping them to regain strength of body and buoyancy of spirit by the sunshine of her loving and sympathetic presence. She loved the cause for which our heroes fought; she loved the soldiers who fought for the sacred cause so dear to her heart. Nor did her love diminish when the cause was lost, and many of the soldiers had fought their last battle and slept their last sleep. The echoes of the last guns of the war had scarcely ceased to reverberate from the Virginian hills, or the islands by the sea, ere she began to arrange for the honorable interment and remembrance of the Southern dead. She travelled from battlefield to battlefield, all over our Southland, gathering up the bones of the dead heroes who were hastily buried where they fell, and brought them to our own city of the dead, and reverently laid them side by side, where, assisted by other loving hands, suitable stones were placed to mark their graves. Nor was this all. In 1866 she organized the first Memorial Association of the South, and ever since, year by year, on the anniversary of the death of Stonewall Jackson, the men, women and children of this City by the Sea make their pilgrimage to beautiful Magnolia to aid this band of noble women in laying tributes upon the graves of those soldiers whose bones she gathered from the widely distant fields where they fell. In addition to the magnificent monument erected mainly through her instrumentality, in the centre of this ground consecrated to heroic dead, she has erected one for the living, in our city, and the Confederate Home of Charleston, in educating the children and the children's children, to remote generations of those who gave their lives in defence of our homes, will be her grandest monument.

With sorrowful hearts, be it, therefore,

Resolved, That in the death of Mrs. Snowden this Chapter has lost one of its most esteemed and honored members, and not only have our city and State been bereaved, but our entire Southland as well.

Resolved, That our tenderest sympathy be extended to her children, who now have only the fragrant memory of their mother's noble character to comfort them in their grief.

Resolved, That this Chapter will wear a badge of mourning on next Memorial Day in honor to her memory.

Resolved, That a blank page in the Minutes be inscribed to her memory; that a copy of these resolutions be sent her children, and they be published in The News and Courier.

Resolved, That this Chapter will assist the Ladies' Memorial Association each year in making wreaths for Memorial Day, and will attend the services at Magnolia Cemetery and aid in the decoration of the soldiers' graves.

March the 27th, 1898. "The State" newspaper had this editorial notice :

"The recent death of this highly esteemed and public-spirited lady has evoked a general expression of sympathy and regret from pulpit and press in the city which was the field of her wonderful achievements.

In her early life bright, vivacious and prominent in social life, she it was who organized and led to success the "'Ladies' Calhoun Monument Association." By her able management and assiduous work in the decade 1850-60, a very large sum had been accumulated (between $40,000 and $50,000) when the war began, and delayed the memorial work. It was a period of daily anxieties to save the fund, and when Charleston was to be abandoned, and there was no place of secure deposit, this devoted lady and her sister took the stocks and bonds into their own custody, and carried them to Columbia, where they were on that dreadful night of 17th of February, 1865, when the torch was applied, and our beautiful city burned. One of the striking incidents of that conflagration was the presence of these two Carolina ladies amid the flames of the burning city, with this large sum of trust securities on their persons. It is needless to say that the whole fund was saved. When war ended, and want was everywhere in the Southland, this good lady founded the "Confederate Home and School," without means, but with a large measure of faith and hope. The extensive property on Broad Street, in Charleston, first rented, and subsequently bought and paid for, and a considerable endowment fund, represent the achievements of her later life."

The members of Camp Sumter, No. 250, U. C. V., formerly "The Survivors' Association of Charleston District," formed in 1866, did not take steps to pass resolutions upon Mrs. Snowden's death until they met in annual session, April 12th, "Fort Sumter Day," thus giving additional force to their action by the large and representative meeting of Confederate Veterans.

The resolutions were offered by Col. James G. Holmes, after some introductory remarks, and seconded by Col. James Armstrong, in a few feeling and fitting words:

Mrs. Mary Amarinthia Snowden having proved her right to the highest respect and reverence, and to the warmest affection of those who fought or suffered for the Confederate States by her life-work, is no less entitled in death to have her good and great deeds commemorated and preserved for pos-. terity. Gifted and self-forgetting type of the South Carolina

Confederate woman, spending and being spent for those, and "The Cause" she loved better than her life, for four years of war, she lived only to minister to Confederate soldiers and sailors, on the field and in the hospitals, and for thirty-three years of peace she strove to care for the wounded and homeless Confederate Veterans, and to protect their mothers, wives and sisters, and to educate their daughters, and from far and near to gather the dead heroes of the Confederacy, that in honored graves they might rest in their own loved Southland, and to build monuments, (the noblest of them all, "The Home for Mothers, Widows and Daughters of Confederate Soldiers and Sailors," in this city) to teach the lessons they died for.   Therefore, be it

Resolved, That Camp Sumter, No. 250, U. C. V., the mother of Confederate Survivors' Associations, as Mrs. Snowden was the first inspiration of Confederate Memorial Associations, having testified by attendance at her funeral to her worth, now places upon a page of the Minute Book this testimony of our reverence and affection for her memory:

Mary Amarinthia Snowden, overborne by service for her loved Confederate sisters and brothers, the living and the dead, laid her down to sleep, February 23rd, 1898.
"Faithful unto death—this her glory."

  *   *   *   *   *   *

> "We chant no requiem where she's sleeping,
> Nor cry "Alas!" with sorrow's breath;
> We send our triumph song to Heaven,
> And this its music—faithful unto death."

"The Evening Post," of Charleston, S. C., said editorially:

"Not long ago we printed a sketch of Mrs. Mary A. Snowden, of Charleston, whose deeds of kindness and mercy during the cruel days of strife and bloodshed in her native city, were told with loving emphasis, and whose work in the establish-

ment of the Confederate Home, and in the erection of the
Confederate Monument in beautiful Magnolia, was also por-
trayed in loving colors. This sketch has only preceded the
death of Mrs. Snowden a short time, as her pure spirit has
ascended to the skies and entered upon a bliss that is immortal.
Her consecrated and unselfish life will be the guiding star for
Charleston maidens and matrons in the coming years, and her
unflinching patriotism is an enduring example to the citizens
of South Carolina. Her memory will be cherished, and her
deeds will be fragrant in other generations."

The following is the sketch referred to above:

September 10th, 1897. Mrs. Mary Amarinthia Snowden
celebrated her 78th birthday. Mrs. Snowden is the daughter
of Joseph Yates, and the widow of William Snowden, M. D.,
of Charleston, S. C. In her ever hospitable home in the city
that first sounded the tocsin of the Confederate War, Mrs.
Snowden still lives, and though for some months she has been
confined to her room, and perhaps may never again go about
doing good and relieving suffering, yet when the Master calls
she will be cheerfully ready, and her works will live after
her. It is peculiarly fitting that a pen and ink sketch of Mrs.
Snowden's life should be framed, in a paper, in her own
home, that is true to the sacred past, for she is a Confederate
woman of Confederate women, and no woman living or dead
has exceeded her in effort or accomplishment for "The Cause"
while it lasted, for the principle as it lives in the persons of
Confederate Veterans and their children, for the memories
that to her are sacred, and of life a part. During the war
Mrs. Snowden, assisted by her equally devoted sister, Mrs.
Isabella Snowden, gave her entire time to the service of the
hospitals, and to nursing the sick and wounded wherever
found, ministering even with Godlike charity to those vandal
soldiers of the Union Army who were laying waste the homes
of those she loved, desecrating the graves of her dead, and
making life a thing to dread for the women of the South.

3

Mrs. Snowden's whole life has been lived unselfishly. She was the inspiration and prime worker of the Calhoun Monument Association, that had accumulated some $75,000 before the war to build a monument to the greatest, purest and most liberal statesman America had produced since Washington, and it was Mrs. Snowden who sewed into her skirts the securities when Sherman burnt Columbia, and preserved the means that enabled the Calhoun Monument Association to erect the imposing monument that now adorns Marion Square, in front of the South Carolina Military Academy, known as the Citadel. The war ended, and Mrs. Snowden and her sister, both widows, turned to mend their grief by continuing to live for others. A brave Marylander, by the name of Charles E. Rodman, who had been paralyzed from his waist down, by being entombed under the falling rampart of Battery Wagener, was the first object of their solicitude, and they took him to their home and ministered unto him until he was removed to St. Philip's Church Home (Episcopal) where he lived, until of necessity removed to the hospital to end his brave life. Then the cry came up from the penniless, wounded, and almost disheartened Confederate Veterans: "Who will aid us to educate our children?" and who but the Snowden widowed sisters answered: "We will." A large and commodious building, occupying a most advantageous position on Broad Street, the principal east and west street of the city, and running back some hundreds of feet to Chalmers Street, was obtained for $1,800 a year, and the sisters Snowden mortgaged the home over their heads, and the only protection for Mrs. M. A. Snowden's two young children, to secure the first year's rental. As I am not writing a history of the Confederate Home, I will only write of it as its institution, growth, maintenance and good work is part of the life, if not the whole life, of Mrs. M. A. Snowden, assisted by her untiring, if less aggressive sister. Mrs. Snowden went to warm-hearted, sympathetic Baltimore to learn how similar eleemosynary institutions were managed, and to obtain aid from those who were well to do, and sympathized with the ruined South. Visiting a home for widows in that city, she was offered by one of the dependent inmates $1—the very first voluntary offer to the cause—and declining, because of the necessities of the giver, was asked if she rejected the widow's mite, replying that she would gratefully accept it then as the seed corn, blessed of God, for her enterprise. The incident got into the papers, and was read in Europe by the helplessly ill daughter (Miss Louise) of the great philanthropist, Hon. W. W. Corcoran, and after the daughter's death the father sent Mrs. M. A. Snowden $1,000, and thus the Confederate Home of Charleston, S. C., the first of its kind, was started to shelter and care for the "mothers, widows and daughters of Confederate soldiers," and to educate the daughters in the faith their brave fathers had fought for, and their womanly mothers had suffered for. It was in 1867 that the Home took shape and being, and if educating the daughters of noble men and women to become self-helping, self-respecting and working women in the world is a good work, then Mary Amarinthia Snowden's name should be illuminated by history, and live in song and story, and in the hearts of grateful people; for some fifteen hundred girls of the State have been educated in the Home for the Mothers, Widows and Daughters of Confederate Soldiers, and Mrs. M. A. Snowden, by her untiring efforts, has caused the establishment, support, and partial endowment of this Home.

Mr. W. W. Corcoran, after a visit to the Home, gave it an additional amount of $5,000, and a generous Baltimore woman has given it, through Mrs. Snowden, $20,000. Surely if to care for sick and wounded Confederate soldiers for four years, and for those dearer to them than life, their mothers, wives and daughters, for thirty years, is entitled to "well done, thou good and faithful servant," then does Mrs. Mary Amarinthia Snowden stand second to no other Confederate woman, and Chapters of Daughters of the Confederacy should be named for her in every State of the late Confederate

States. For a high-spirited, dauntless woman, full of life and human frailties, to live a long, useful and unselfish life for others, and those others endeared to her only by their humanity, is Christlike, and Mary Amarinthia Snowden's cross will burgeon into the crown promised of Him. Mrs. Snowden formed, it is believed, the first Memorial Association in the South, 1866, and with singular propriety, it adopted the anniversary of Stonewall Jackson's death, May 10th, as its memorial day; and since 1866 this day has been observed in Charleston by the Ladies' Memorial Association and the citizens generally, and now that the State has made it a legal holiday, only the selfish money-lovers and those who were faint-hearted in war, and would forget in peace, fail to observe the day. The first general monument to the Confederate dead was unveiled in the soldier's plot in beautiful Magnolia Cemetery. South Carolina's own Wade Hampton delivered the address, and it is not saying too much to affirm that the bronze Confederate soldier, clutching his flag to his breast, as he grasps his rifle with the other hand, shows its Munich birth, and is the most truth-telling and spirited monument in the South, if not in the United States, as it stands guarding the graves of some eight hundred Confederate dead, many of whose bodies were removed from the graves of Gettysburg's battlefield. Mrs. Snowden is the President of the L. M. A., and as long as she is strong enough to sit in a carriage will attend the solemn, and with us always impressive, ceremony of love and admiration, and will see to it, as she has done for thirty-one years, that each and every grave has its evergreen cross and wreath. As Wade Hampton must ever be our typical South Carolina Confederate Soldier, so must Mary Amarinthia Snowden remain the type of the South Carolina Confederate Woman, fearless and faithful.

JAMES G. HOLMES.

We find in The News and Courier of later date, this evidence that Mrs. Snowden was appreciated out of her State, as well as in it, as we read:

"In April last, Col. James G. Holmes visited Nashville, Tenn., to make arrangements for the comfort of the comrades of the South Carolina Division, United Confederate Veterans, who were to attend the re-union of the United Confederate Veterans in June following. Col. Holmes was invited to a meeting of the Nashville Chapter, Daughters of the Confederacy, and was called upon for a speech, of course. Col. Holmes gave an account of the formation of Charleston Chapter, Daughters of the Confederacy, and then he told of the noblest work that has been done in this city, and none more needed or nobler had been done elsewhere at any time. To Mrs. Mary Amarinthia Snowden, and to her sister, the late Mrs. Isabella Snowden, he gave fitting praise for the inception and carrying on of the noble work that for thirty years has furnished a home for many unfortunate ladies of the State, many of them bearing historic names, and not a few of whom had once possessed handsome fortunes and beautiful homes of hospitality. The "Home for the Mothers, Widows and Daughters of Confederate Soldiers" has not only done this, but has enabled some twelve hundred girls, who represented Confederate soldiers, dead and living, to get a good education, and learn domestic habits of neatness and economy, fitting them to become, as many of them have, heads of families that are an honor to the State.

Immediately after Col. Holmes's address, Mrs. Mary Amarinthia Snowden was unanimously elected an honorary member of "Nashville Chapter, Daughters of the Confederacy," but not until yesterday did Col. Holmes receive the certificate that he, as the Chapter's delegated messenger, was requested to present to Mrs. Snowden. The certificate is the regular official certificate of membership, and bears the seal of the Order, and is signed by Mrs. John Overton, Pres-

ident, and Miss Mackie Hardison, Secretary, of Nashville
Chapter, and countersigned by Mrs. Ellen Bernard Lee,
President, and Mrs. John P. Hickman, Secretary of the
U. D. C.; (Mrs. Lee is the wife of General Fitzhugh Lee)
and also by Mrs. M. C. Goodlett, State President. The
inability to obtain the signature of Mrs. Lee until recently has
been the cause of the delay in forwarding the certificate to
Mrs. Snowden, though she was apprised of its coming in
April, from a clipping from the Nashville Banner, that
reported the incident referred to above Col. Holmes presented the certificate to Mrs. Snowden yesterday afternoon at
her home, to which she has been confined for many months.

Mrs. Snowden is a typical "Daughter of the Confederacy,"
and Nashville Chapter has done itself honor in so kindly and
appreciatively recognizing the fact, and this act must ever
serve to bind the Nashville and Charleston Chapters in the
strong bonds of the "United Daughters of the Confederacy,"
especially as Mrs. Snowden is also an honorary member of the
Charleston Chapter "

Except only the "Confederate Home," it was the care of
the graves of Confederate soldiers and sailors that was nearest
Mrs. Snowden's heart; and Memorial Day, May 10th, the
anniversary of Stonewall Jackson's death, always found her
prepared with fresh flowers and evergreen wreaths and crosses
to place upon the lowly Southern Mecca-mounds, that
mother-like, hid from view the dear remains of valiant heroes.
It was most fitting then, that the first Memorial Day after her
death was chosen by the Ladies' Memorial Association as the
proper time to give public exhibition of their sense of loss.
The members of the Association, as also the members of the
Charleston Chapter, United Daughters of the Confederacy,
and the young ladies of the Confederate Home, wore badges
of mourning on the left breast, and part of the simple service
of the day was specially in memory of Mrs. Snowden. After
the opening prayer had been offered by the Rev. Lucius
Cuthbert, D. D., Col. Zimmerman Davis, commanding

Charleston Regiment, U. C. V., presiding, spoke as fol lows :

More than eighteen hundred years ago the founder of Christianity immortalized the name of Mary, when He said of her of Bethany, for the costly and loving service she had rendered Him: "Verily, I say unto you, wheresoever this Gospel shall be preached in the whole world, that also which this woman has done shall be spoken of for a memorial of her."

We pause a moment in these solemn proceedings to-day to recall another Mary, that noble woman who, for more than thirty years, has loved and honored this hallowed spot; by whose loving hands the bones of more than eight hundred valiant Southern heroes have been gathered from the red fields of battle and given tender burial here, and by whose untiring efforts these head stones and that imposing monument have been erected to commemorate their services to their country.

As long as this city of the dead shall remain as the receptacle of mortality, as long as your city of the living shall sit enthroned by the sea, so long will the name of Mary Amarinthia Snowden be honored and revered !

The ladies of the Memorial Association, of which she was the distinguished President during all these years, have requested Col. James G. Holmes to offer a tribute to her memory to-day.

THE TRIBUTE.

Mr. Chairman and Faithful Friends of the Fallen Cause; Memorial Day is meaningful for those of us gathered here to-day reverently to renew our belief in the equity of a cause loved, though lost forever, and to pay tribute, as best we may, to the worth of those silent sleepers who gave their lives in the vain effort to establish the outward manifestation of a principle that is deathless. The softening years in their rhythmic flow through the three decades and more since this beautiful custom we celebrate to-day was first inspired by a brave woman, now sainted, had brought, as only time can, surcease of violent grief, and the sense of exultation that these glorious dead were of our very own, our dead, was akin to the feeling that animates when we lift our hats and bow our heads at the graves of Washington, and of Davis, of Lee, of the John- stons, of Jackson and of Beauregard, or of our own R. H. Anderson, Barnard E. Bee, Clement H. Stevens, Maxey Gregg, Jenkins, Gist and other heroes, who fell upon the fateful field, but to-day the past seems to be compressed into the present, and there would seem to be no future. To-day, again, those graves are open graves, the clods seem falling upon the echoing coffins, and our grief is all renewed, the wounds in our hearts are torn open, and time seems no longer a healer. 'Tis true the sweet May breezes, fraught with a suggestion of the briny deep just beyond, where "the sand beach fastens the fringe of the marsh to the folds of the land," fan our cheeks, the requiem singers of our heroic dead, the mocking birds, sing from these "immemorial oaks;" our typifying soldier still guards with lifelike care the flag of his and our devotion. Why, then, is our sadness renewed? Why do these graves seem freshly dug, ready to hide from us those we reverently love? The same sentiment that makes grief as yet triumph over exultation, when we stand beside the graves of our recently dead Confederate heroes, Kennedy, McKissick, McGowan, Hagood, Bratton, sways us when we look around and ask each other, and our own hearts, where is she?

Where is the typical Confederate woman? She who made this day an assured annual ceremonial of devotion; she who gathered the hallowed dust mingling with Mother Earth in those sacred mounds from far and near, from States that fought and lost, from States that slew and conquered; she that put that soldier on guard to remind the sordid and selfish, and to teach the ignorant and the young, that principle must live e'en though the cause that inspired it perished; she that succored the mother and widow and orphan of Confederate soldiers and sailors, totally forgetful of self, and "In His Name," knowing only one emblazonment for the banner that led her on "Faithful unto the end!" Yes, citizens and soldiers; yes, Confederate Veterans and Sons; yes, Daughters of the Confederacy, and faithful co-workers of the Ladies' Memorial Association; to-day grief must have its sway, for Mary Amarinthia Snowden is no longer of us; her banner, with its emblazoned, inspiring inscription, "Faithful unto the end," has been carried aloft, and with the eyes of faith we see, like Constantine, another Southern Cross in the heavens, and the very stars when they come forth to-night will seem to re-arrange themselves, and not "In hoc signo vinces" flash forth with their lambent rays, but "Faithful unto the end" will stand out from the deep blue of night's heaven, in clustering points of clear star-pointed scintillations, and to the ear of faith Mary Amarinthia and Isabella Snowden's voices will seem to sing in sweet unison from heaven to earth:

"Sisters of the Memorial Association, Daughters of the Confederacy, Confederate Veterans and Sons, never neglect this hallowed spot, never give up this solemn, right-life-teaching custom—be ye "Faithful unto the end," until "we are all re-united." Mary Amarinthia Snowden, and her less aggressive, but none the less faithful sister, Isabella, co-workers always in war and peace for Confederate soldiers and sailors, and those dear to them, sleep just over there, within this same God's acre. It would have seemed appropriate that they should have laid them down to rest at the foot of their monument, guarded by their dead, but as this may not be, why not give them the only monument they would approve of—one that, like the sainted dead, will prove unselfish, and, like their teaching, ennobles. Let every living woman of the eighteen hundred educated at the Confederate Home School organize in every County of the State a "Snowden Sisters' Monument Association," and go to work to collect funds, and by October 1st, 1899, let all moneys made or collected be turned into the treasury of the Confederate Home of this city, to create the "Snowden Sisters' Scholarship Fund" for the Home, and let steps be taken at once to change the name of the Home to "The Snowden Sisters' Memorial Home for the Mothers, Widows and Daughters of Confederate Soldiers and Sailors." Then into the front of the building put another tablet, with the words "Snowden Sisters' Memorial," so that the inscription complete will read: "Snowden Sisters' Memorial Confederate Home." Only in this way can the memory of the devoted sisters be preserved, serving to teach a lesson to this and coming generations, and a monument to their memory be created that would not give offence to the now sainted dead.

MARY AMARINTHIA SNOWDEN.

" Faithful unto death—this her glory,
    And this the record of her days;
No brighter guerdon can we give her,
    Nor words of nobler praise.

She asked not where the prize was golden,
    She went where duty led;
And where the need of help was greatest,
    Thither her footsteps sped.

Love held her in its chains forever,
    And friendship in a close embrace;
To every call of duty and of honor
    She turned a smiling face.

She clung the closer when misfortune darkened,
    She cared not for the worldlings' scorn;
And to the sad and weary hearted
    She brought a brighter morn.

We chant no requiem where she's sleeping,
    Nor cry "Alas!" with sorrow's breath;
We send our triumph song to heaven,
    And this its music—faithful unto death."

COL. WILLIAM ELLIOTT.

Col. Davis next introduced Col. William Elliott, saying: "I have the honor and the pleasure of announcing that the Ladies' Memorial Association has secured, as orator of the day, the gallant soldier, the wise statesman, our Representative in Congress, the Hon. William Elliott. He needs no introduction to this audience."

Col. Elliott rose and spoke as follows:

Mr. Chairman and Ladies of the Memorial Association: After the lapse of a third of a century from that fateful season when the Confederate Cause went down in defeat, we once more meet to pay tribute to our dead. A generation has passed away, another has come upon the scene, new men have taken the places of those whose faces were once so familiar to us, moderate prosperity has long ago succeeded to the fearful trials and privations that the war left behind it, another war is upon us, and yet, as the years follow each other in their stately course, and bring to us this blessed day, whatever else may be forgotten or neglected, this pious pilgrimage is ever remembered. Other people celebrate victories; we pay tribute to defeated valor. Others crown their heroes with laurels, while enjoying the rich fruits of successful war; we deck the graves of our glorious dead in humble thankfulness that we were once permitted to stand with them, and with willing determination to endure without a murmur, whatever their and our cause entailed. In other parts of the world governments erect monuments to their soldiers, and organize celebrations to perpetuate their achievements; here gentle women, stirred by sacred promptings, forever keep alive the memory of our fallen heroes.

All honor to the heroic women of the South! With bleeding hearts, but with smiling faces, they sent their loved ones to the front, and throughout the conflict cheered them on by their unconquerable spirit. They ministered to the sick, nursed the wounded, applauded the brave, and sent the laggard to the field. They bore every privation with cheerful determination. If there was a luxury to be had, it was for the soldier, not for themselves. They devoted their lives to the cause, and what their deft, nimble fingers found to do, can never be realized save by those who lived in that heroic age.

When the war was over, and defeat had overtaken their cause, and their hopes were crushed, they did not falter or despair, but with brave hearts braced themselves for the stern duties of the hour. Although encompassed by the narrow and remorseless pressure of actual poverty, no sooner had they accustomed themselves to tread the hard and rough road, than their unquenchable devotion to the Confederate Cause welled up in deeds of tender care for the graves of their heroic dead, and merciful provision for their helpless families.

Chief in this good work was this grand old city, and foremost in this city was the dear lady whose loss we mourn to-day. Tireless in devotion, unflagging in zeal, boundless in self-sacrifice, she wrought as much honor for Charleston as did the brave men whose memory she cherished.

I can add nothing to the glowing tribute just pronounced. I speak to-day by her command—the highest honor ever done me. The Confederate Home is a noble monument to her memory. But noble as that is, there must be no halting on the part of this people in lifting to the skies the shaft that the gratitude and love of her sisters have already commenced to rear.

The "Confederate Veteran," of Nashville, Tenn., published in its July, 1898, number, the verses below under this caption:

MRS. MARY AMARINTHIA SNOWDEN,

(Founder of the "Home for Mothers, Widows and Daughters of Confederate Soldiers and Sailors.")

BY HULDA LEIGH.

"Most potent force, a noble life—
  A gracious star whose life doth go
Through unknown ages softly, rife
  With beauty that doth add halo.
This fearless, patriotic life
  Was spent that others strong might grow.

For youth's great need, the homeless old.
  Her great, deep heart, did beat always;
Ne'er chilled by poverty's white cold,
  True, brave and strong through all the days.
She culture placed in deathless mold,
  A shaft should nobly speak her praise."

At the Annual Re-union of the South Carolina Division, United Confederate Veterans, held in Charleston, April 27th to 29th, 1898, Col. James G. Holmes "paid a glowing tribute to the memory of the women of the Confederacy, and especially to Mrs. Mary Amarinthia Snowden, as a woman who had done as much, or more, for the Confederate Cause than any other. He asked that the Adjutant-General of the Division be instructed to have a page in the Minutes inscribed to her memory, and that the action of the Major-General commanding, in attending officially her funeral, with his Staff, be recorded for those who come after:—so ordered."

"Major-General C. Irvine Walker, the Division Commander, presiding, referring to the above, recalled an incident of Bragg's Kentucky campaign." He said: "When we got into Tennessee, the men were ordered to take off knapsacks, and we took what we could in our blankets, which eventually all came to. When we returned from Kentucky, I don't think any man in the regiment had a whole suit of clothes, pair of shoes, or any other serviceable article of clothing. When we reached Knoxville there was an abundant supply of clothes and shoes, and everything the South Carolina troops needed, sent by Mrs. M. A. Snowden."

The editor of this memorial pamphlet has endeavored to collect all of the eulogies published in honor of Mrs. Snowden. Doubtless many have not come under his notice, nor been seen by her children, Miss May Snowden and Mr. Yates Snowden, who have aided him in making the collection.

It is not in the scope of the resolution, inviting the most willing laborer to his congenial task, that he of himself should write anything, and hence he has endeavored merely to produce a Mosaic that preserves the unities.

In closing this pleasant, if sadly solemn work, he must, however, be allowed to do for the readers, who knew them, or of them, what death has done in transporting to Paradise and re-uniting Mary Amarinthia and Isabella S. Snowden, sisters in the flesh, true sisters in faith and good works. Christ's beatitude be theirs, and "Ye! our own proud Palmettoes, with your heads, like theirs, glory crowned, sentinel their graves; and Oh! ye "immemorial oaks," with your swaying mosses, woo the sea-salted breezes from Sumter-guarded ocean, with their soulful monotones, to diapason all nature's sweet sounds, to cadence with the angelic notes of the requiem-singing mocking birds, when they, at Vespers' holy hour, chant above the resting place of the sainted sisters twain, 'till the sentinel stars swing in their orbits, and God's peace rests over all.

The Ladies' Memorial Association invites the co-operation of the Alumni of the Confederate Home School, and of all others friendly to the education of female descendants of Confederate soldiers and sailors, to contribute to the fund to create the " Snowden Sisters' Scholarship," now well advanced, and thus, as those life-workers would have wished it, memorialize them in death, so that their works may continue after them, e'en as they were "faithful unto death—this their glory."